My Best Friend's a Genius

George Ivanoff
Toby Quarmby

Australia • Brazil • Japan • Korea • Mexico • Singapore • Spain • United Kingdom • United States

My Best Friend's a Genius

Fast Forward
Gold Level 21

Text: George Ivanoff
Illustrations: Toby Quarmby
Editor: Johanna Rohan
Design: Karen Mayo
Series design: James Lowe
Production controller: Seona Galbally
Audio recordings: Juliet Hill, Picture Start
Spoken by: Matthew King and Abbe Holmes
Reprint: Siew Han Ong

ISBN 978 0 17 012672 4
ISBN 978 0 17 012669 4 (set)

Cengage Learning Australia
Level 7, 80 Dorcas Street
South Melbourne, Victoria Australia 3205
Phone: 1300 790 853

Cengage Learning New Zealand
Unit 4B Rosedale Office Park
331 Rosedale Road, Albany, North Shore NZ 0632
Phone: 0508 635 766

For learning solutions, visit cengage.com.au

Printed in Australia by Ligare Pty Ltd
7 8 9 10 11 12 13 20 19 18 17 16

Evaluated in independent research by staff from the Department of Language, Literacy and Arts Education at the University of Melbourne.

My Best Friend's a Genius

George Ivanoff
Toby Quarmby

Contents

The Boy Genius

Miles is a genius!
That means that he's *really* smart –
super brainy!
He invents things . . . weird things,
things you think will never work,
but they always do.
He invents things like flying skateboards,
computer-controlled mouse-traps
and automatic toilet flushers.

How do I know this?
Miles is my best friend.

My name is Gary.
I'm not a genius.
I don't invent things.
But, I'm good at helping Miles
get out of trouble.
That's another thing that Miles
is good at – getting into trouble.
Well . . . it's his inventions that get him
into trouble.

The automatic toilet flusher scared
Miles's mum so much
that she grounded him for a week.

Let me tell you about the time
Miles made a hyper phone.

Yes, that's right, a hyper phone.
He sent me out to get the parts
he needed for the phone.
This was going to be his best-ever
invention.
It was, sort of.

The Hyper Phone

What's a hyper phone?
It's a mobile phone that
lets you talk to aliens.

Miles read this feature article
about UFOs –
Unidentified Flying Objects –
and he was sure that UFOs
are spaceships from another planet.

Anyway, he decided to talk to
the aliens in the UFOs.

"It won't work," I said when Miles
told me about it.
"A phone's no good unless there's
another phone to ring.
Why would aliens have mobile phones?"

"If aliens can build spaceships that come
to Earth," explained Miles,
"they must have mobile phones.
It's logical!"

I didn't think it was logical,
but there's no arguing with Miles.
I just went and got what he needed.

It took Miles three days to make a little box with flashing lights on it. When I saw it for the first time, I just nodded and said, "That's great."

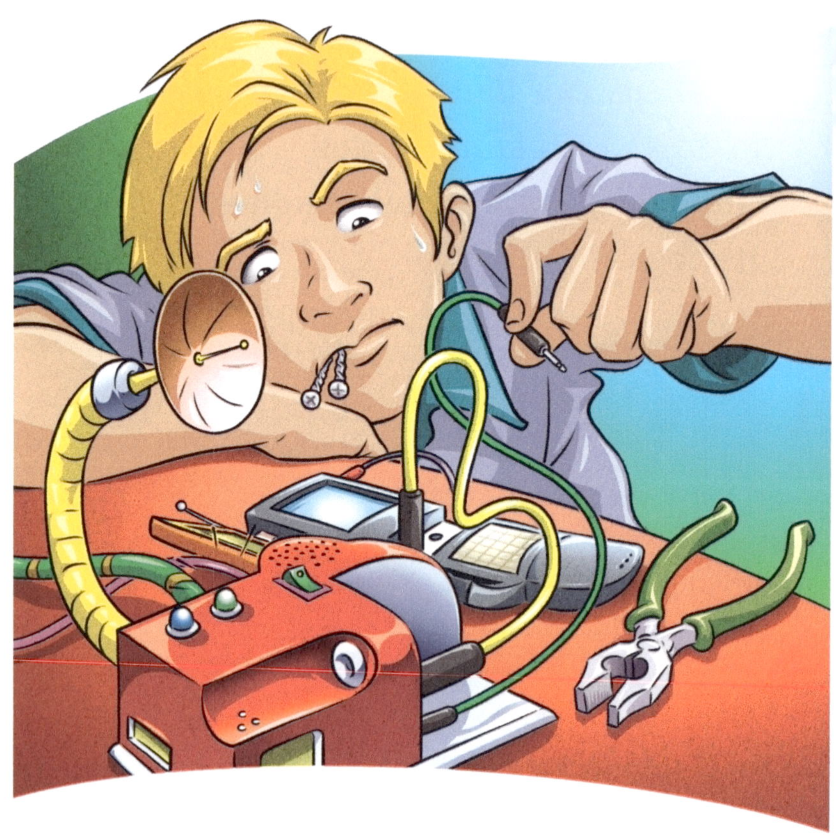

Then, Miles got out his mobile phone and plugged it into the box.

Miles has a weird-looking
mobile phone.
His parents wouldn't buy him one,
so he made one himself.
It works really well,
and calls don't cost anything,
but it looks like something out of
a sci-fi movie.

"Now what?" I asked Miles.

"I'm not sure," he said, shrugging his shoulders. "I don't know what number to ring."

"You're joking," I said.

Miles just shook his head sadly
and closed his eyes.
I thought he was going to cry.
Suddenly, his eyes snapped open.
"I've got it!" he said.
"I'll use the computer to quickly ring
numbers until we get an alien
on the phone."

"That could take ages," I said.

Miles looked sad again …
but then the light on his desk
started to go on and off,
and his mobile phone rang …

Chapter 3

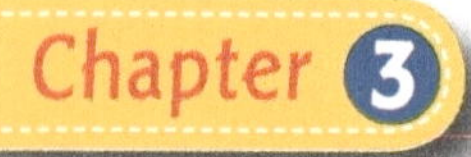

Talking to Aliens?

Miles pressed the speaker phone button.
A high-pitched, squeaky sound came out of the phone.

"What is that?" I asked.

"I think that's an alien," answered Miles.

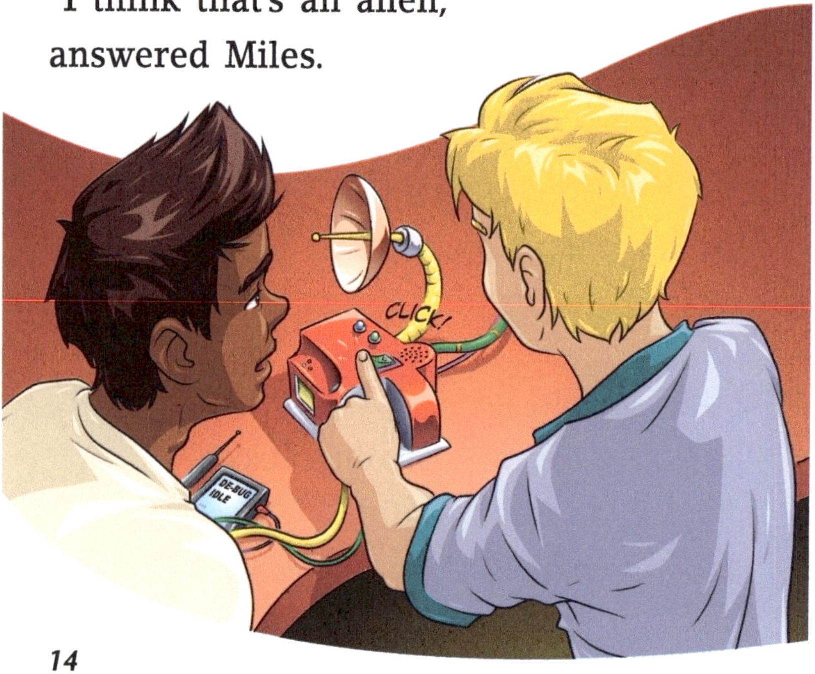

More strange sounds came from the phone.

"But …" I looked at Miles. "What's the point of ringing aliens if we can't understand what they're saying?"

There was a crackle of electricity around the box, and the desk light went on and off again.
Slowly, the strange squeaky sounds turned into words.

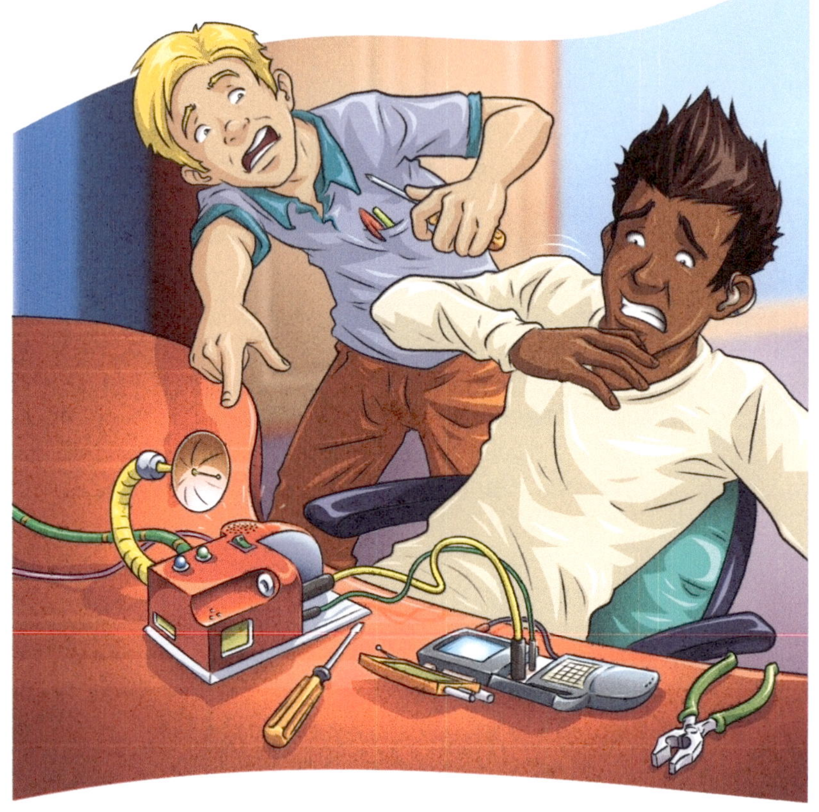

"Who are you and where are you from?" said a voice.

"My name is Miles,"
said Miles, excitedly.
"I'm from Earth.
This is my friend Gary.
He's also from Earth."

"I know you're from Earth,"
said the voice.
"I mean, what part of Earth
are you in?"

"Australia," I said.

"Australia?" asked the voice.

"What about you?" asked Miles.
"What planet are you from?"

"Planet?" replied the voice.
"I'm on Earth."

"You're not an alien?"
I asked.

"Alien?" laughed the voice.
"No. I'm a scientist.
I'm at the Antarctic research base."

Miles looked really disappointed. Suddenly, there was a huge crackle of electricity around the box and phone, and all the lights in the house went off.

"Miles!" called a voice from downstairs. "What have you done now?"

"My mum," said Miles, heading for the door. "I'd better calm her down."

Chapter 4

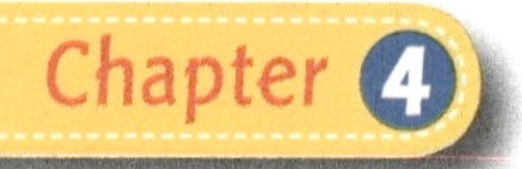

The Future

As Miles left the room,
the voice on the phone asked,
"You say you're from Australia?"

"Yes," I replied.

"But Australia doesn't exist any more.
It became a part of the Oceanic Republic
over 100 years ago."

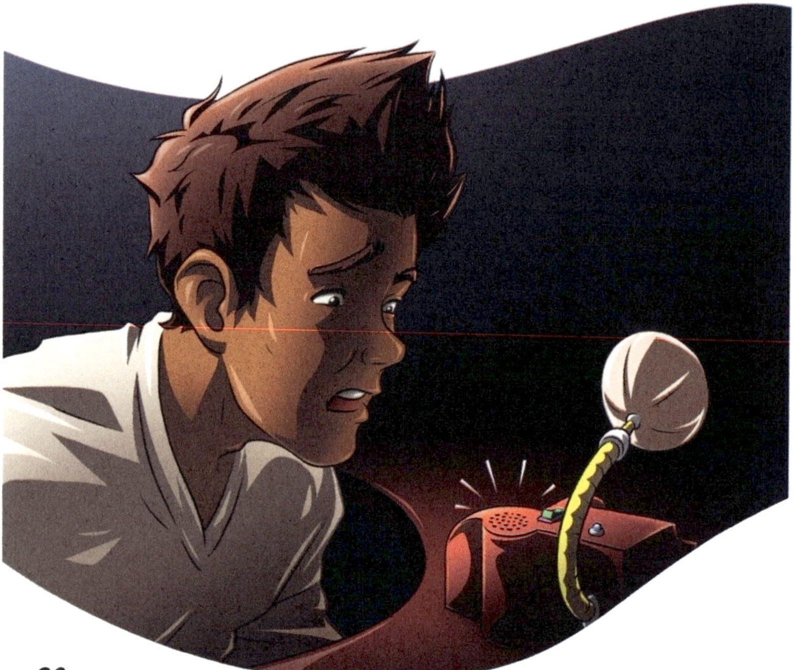

"What?" I shouted.
Then I calmed down
and controlled my voice.
"What … what year is it?"

"Year?" asked the voice.
"It's 2156, of course.
That's a very strange thing to ..."

Suddenly, there was another crackle of electricity and the phone went dead.
I grabbed it and looked at the buttons.
Yes!
There was one called 'last number'.
I pressed it and waited.
"I'm sorry," said a strange voice,
"but the number you are trying to reach is unavailable.
Please try again later."

I heard yelling from downstairs.
Oh well, I thought,
time to go help Miles get out
of trouble –
again!